For my fierce, loving mom, Barbara
—JD

To Rowen and Tallulah
—CD

ABOUT THIS BOOK

The illustrations for this book were done digitally with Procreate. This book was edited by Christy Ottaviano and designed by Patrick Collins with art direction from Saho Fujii. The production was supervised by Lillian Sun, and the production editor was Annie McDonnell. The text was set in Adoquin, and the display type is Barmbrack.

Good Dream Dragon

By **JACKY DAVIS**

Illustrated by **COURTNEY DAWSON**

Christy Ottaviano Books

LITTLE, BROWN AND COMPANY

New York Boston

Once upon a bedtime,
after the sky had turned
a dusky blue,

a child was asked
to put on their pj's,

brush their teeth,

and go to bed.

Before they knew it, a book had been read. Kisses given. Then there was a click, and off went the light.

"Sweet dreams," said Momma. "Good night."

"I'm afraid of bad dreams!" cried the child.

"If you need to, you can always call on the Good Dream Dragon!" reassured Momma.

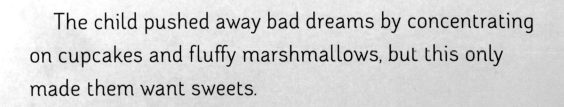

The child pushed away bad dreams by concentrating on cupcakes and fluffy marshmallows, but this only made them want sweets.

Then they tried counting sheep to help fall asleep.
When that didn't work, they counted ducks, cows, and pigs
until their head was filled with baaing, quacking, mooing,
oinking, and even the crow of a rooster.

Now very awake, the child worried that they would never
find their good dreams.

Unless . . .

. . . it was time to call the Good Dream Dragon.
Reaching for the flashlight they used to read under
the blanket, the child flashed signals into the dark
sky, summoning the dragon.

They waited, but there was no response. Maybe
the Good Dream Dragon couldn't see the light
through the clouds?

So the child called out loudly and clearly, "Good
Dream Dragon, I need you now!"

Hearing the child's call, the Good Dream Dragon burst into the quiet room with a majestic SHWISSHHHH and a fantastic SHWOOSHHHH.

"If your good dreams aren't coming to you," said the dragon, "I will bring you to them!"

The Good Dream Dragon folded her wings around
the child and took flight, flying up into the sky,
higher and higher, until they were weaving through
the stars. They scooped up stardust and painted the
inky-black sky with light.

After racing past comets and chasing
shooting stars, they eventually glided
into the Good Dream Galaxy and landed
on a mountaintop in Dreamland.

"We're here!" declared the dragon.

They tumbled down to the edge of a stream
where a giant teapot filled with ginger tea
awaited them.

The child skipped cookies
like stones over the surface
of the water.

Musical notes fell softly from pillowy clouds, forming a lullaby. The child hopped onto a sound wave and surfed across the land, all the way to a town that was built entirely of books.

FAIRYTALES

There, the child found a cushy chair stuffed with bedtime stories. They discovered a story about a child who, with the help of a dragon, went searching through vast galaxies to find their good dreams.

Soon the child's eyes began to feel heavy, and they yawned. The dragon decided that it was time to go home, and they soared silently back to their world.

When the child recognized their planet,
they thought it looked more magical than
Dreamland, and when they saw their house
wrapped in silvery moonlight, they thought it
looked like a dream . . .

...and when they plopped down into their bed, they felt like they were floating on the softest cloud.

"I have to leave now," said the Good Dream Dragon.

"Wait," insisted the child. "I need you to stay with me!"

"You don't need me anymore," replied the dragon. "You've proven your courage by traveling through the night sky on the wings of a dragon."

The child agreed that they had been very brave and that they were able to find their own good dreams.

"Good night," sighed the child, snuggling under their heavy blanket.

"Whenever you need me," whispered the Good Dream Dragon, "just call my name!"